MW01140127

Phonics Friends

Pam's Trip to the Park
The Sound of P

The Child's World

By Joanne Meier and Cecilia Minden

The Child's World

Published in the United States of America
by The Child's World®
PO Box 326
Chanhassen, MN 55317-0326
800-599-READ
www.childsworld.com

The Child's World®: Mary Berendes, Publishing Director

Editorial Directions, Inc.: E. Russell Primm, Editorial Director
and Project Editor; Katie Marsico, Associate Editor; Judith
Shiffer, Associate Editor and School Media Specialist;
Linda S. Koutris, Photo Researcher and Selector

The Design Lab: Kathleen Petelinsek, Design and Page
Production

Photographs ©: Corbis: cover, 10, 12, 18;
Corbis/Macduff Everton: 8; Corbis/Robert Holmes: 4;
Flanagan Publishing Services: 20; Getty Images/Brand X
Pictures/Triolo Productions/Burke: 16; Getty Images/
Geostock: 14; Photo Edit, Inc./Michael Newman: 6.

Copyright © 2005 by The Child's World®
All rights reserved. No part of this book may be
reproduced or utilized in any form or by any means
without written permission from the publisher.

Library of Congress Cataloging-in-Publication Data
Meier, Joanne D.
    Pam's trip to the park : the sound of P / by Joanne
Meier and Cecilia Minden.
        p. cm. — (Phonics friends)
    Summary: Simple text featuring the sound of the letter
"p" tells about Pam's adventures in the park.
    ISBN 1-59296-302-1 (library bound : alk. paper)
    [1. English language—Phonetics. 2. Reading.] I. Minden,
Cecilia. II. Title. III. Series.
PZ7.M5148Pam 2004
[E]—dc22   2004002237

Note to parents and educators:

The Child's World® has created Phonics Friends with the goal of exposing children to engaging stories and pictures that assist in phonics development. The books in the series will help children learn the relationships between the letters of written language and the individual sounds of spoken language. This contact helps children learn to use these relationships to read and write words.

The books in this series follow a similar format. An introductory page, to be read by an adult, introduces the child to the phonics feature, or sound, that will be highlighted in the book. Read this page to the child, stressing the phonic feature. Help the student learn how to form the sound with her mouth. The Phonics Friends story and engaging photographs follow the introduction. At the end of the story, word lists categorize the feature words into their phonic element. Additional information on using these lists is on The Child's World® Web site listed at the top of this page.

Each book in this series has been carefully written to meet specific readability requirements. Close attention has been paid to elements such as word count, sentence length, and vocabulary. Readability formulas measure the ease with which the text can be read and understood. Each Phonics Friends book has been analyzed using the Spache readability formula. For more information on this formula, as well as the levels for each of the books in this series please visit The Child's World® Web site.

Reading research suggests that systematic phonics instruction can greatly improve students' word recognition, spelling, and comprehension skills. The Phonics Friends series assists in the teaching of phonics by providing students with important opportunities to apply their knowledge of phonics as they read words, sentences, and text.

This is the letter *p*.

In this book, you will read words that have the *p* sound as in:

park, pie, pet, and *pen.*

Pam is at the park.

Dad packed a lunch.

Mom made a pie.

This park has a petting zoo.

There are lots of animals to pet.

Some animals are in a pen.

The pigs are in a pen.

The pigs are hard to pick up.

Pam will just pet the pigs.

The goats are in a bigger pen.

Pam has a pail of goat food.

There is a chicken in the last pen.

It picks at the pan of food.

Pam's family finds the

perfect place for a picnic.

The pie is the best part.

After lunch, Pam and her parents play on the grass.

Let's go pet the pigs again.

"Good-bye, park! Good-bye, pigs!" says Pam.

Fun Facts

Yellowstone National Park is the oldest national park in the United States. This park is located in parts of Wyoming, Montana, and Idaho. Yellowstone Park is home to the Little Grand Canyon, as well as many kinds of wildlife including bear, buffalo, and wolves. But not all parks are known for their natural wonders. Central Park in Manhattan, New York, is located in the middle of a major city. This park features a museum, zoo, ice-skating rink, theater, playgrounds, fountains, and many other attractions.

Have you ever wondered why pigs like to roll around in the mud? When dogs are hot, they pant. Human beings sweat. To stay cool, pigs take a bath in the mud. This lowers their body temperature and also protects them from getting sunburned or bitten by insects.

Activity

Visiting Pigs at the Petting Zoo

If you like pigs and other animals, consider visiting a petting zoo. Petting zoos usually give you a chance to see certain farm animals up close. You may even get to pet or feed a pig! If you're lucky, you might also see other animals such as goats, sheep, cows, and chickens.

To Learn More

Books
About the Sound of P
Flanagan, Alice K. *A Pet: The Sound of P.* Chanhassen, Minn.: The Child's World, 2000.

About Parks
Capucilli, Alyssa Satin, and Par Schories (illustrator). *Biscuit Goes to the Park.* New York: HarperFestival, 2002.

Day, Alexandra. *Carl's Afternoon in the Park.* New York: Farrar, Straus & Giroux, 1991.

Domeniconi, David, and Pam Carroll (illustrator). *M Is for Majestic: A National Parks Alphabet.* Chelsea, Mich.: Sleeping Bear Press, 2003.

About Pigs
Falconer, Ian. *Olivia.* New York: Atheneum Books for Young Readers, 2000.

Numeroff, Laura, and Felicia Bond (illustrator). *If You Give a Pig a Pancake.* New York: Laura Geringer Books, 1998.

Trivizas, Eugene, and Helen Oxenbury (illustrator). *The Three Little Wolves and the Big Bad Pig.* New York: Margaret K. McElderry Books, 1993.

Web Sites
Visit our home page for lots of links about the Sound of P:

http://www.childsworld.com/links.html

Note to Parents, Teachers, and Librarians: We routinely check our Web links to make sure they're safe, active sites—so encourage your readers to check them out!

P Feature Words

Proper Names
Pam

Feature Words in Initial Position
pack
pail
pan
parent
park
part
pen
perfect
pet
petting
pick
picnic
pie
pig

Feature Word in Final Position
up

Feature Words with Blend
place
play

About the Authors

Joanne Meier, PhD, has worked as an elementary school teacher and university professor. She earned her BA in early childhood education from the University of South Carolina, and her MEd and PhD in education from the University of Virginia. She currently works as a literacy consultant for schools and private organizations. Joanne Meier lives with her husband Eric, and spends most of her time chasing her two daughters, Kella and Erin, and her two cats, Sam and Gilly, in Charlottesville, Virginia.

Cecilia Minden, PhD, directs the Language and Literacy Program at the Harvard Graduate School of Education. She is a reading specialist with classroom and administrative experience in grades K–12. She earned her PhD in reading education from the University of Virginia. Cecilia and her husband Dave Cupp enjoy sharing their love of reading with their granddaughter Chelsea.